J954
AUNG SAN SUU KYI.
LET'S VISIT NEPAL

LET'S VISIT NEPAL

Let's visit NEPAL

AUNG SAN SUU KYI

First published 1985
© Aung San Suu Kyi 1985
All rights reserved. No part of this publication may be reproduced, stored in a retrieval system, or transmitted, in any form or by any means, electronic, mechanical, photocopying, recording or otherwise, without the prior permission of Burke Publishing Company Limited.

Allen County Public Library
Ft. Wayne, Indiana

ACKNOWLEDGEMENTS

The Author and Publishers are grateful to the following organizations and individuals for permission to reproduce copyright photographs in this book:
Michael Aris; I. Bruce/IMAG; Hewett Street Studios; E. J. Leetham/IMAG; Eugénie Peter.

CIP data
Aung San Suu Kyi
  Let's visit Nepal
    1. Nepal – Social life and customs – Juvenile Literature
    I. Title
  954.9'6   DS493.7

ISBN 0 222 00981 0

Burke Publishing Company Limited
Pegasus House, 116-120 Golden Lane, London EC1Y 0TL, England.
Burke Publishing (Canada) Limited
Registered Office: 20 Queen Street West, Suite 3000, Box 30, Toronto, Canada M5H 1V5.
Burke Publishing Company Inc.
Registered Office: 333 State Street, PO Box 1740, Bridgeport, Connecticut 06601, U.S.A.
Filmset in Baskerville by Graphiti (Hull) Ltd., Hull, England.
Printed in Singapore by Tien Wah Press (Pte.) Ltd.

2261819

Contents

	Page
A Himalayan Kingdom	7
The World's Only Hindu Monarchy	17
Entering the Modern World	28
Worshipping the Gods	36
A Medley of Peoples	49
The Valley of Kathmandu	62
Exploring the Country	76
Facing the Future	87
Index	93

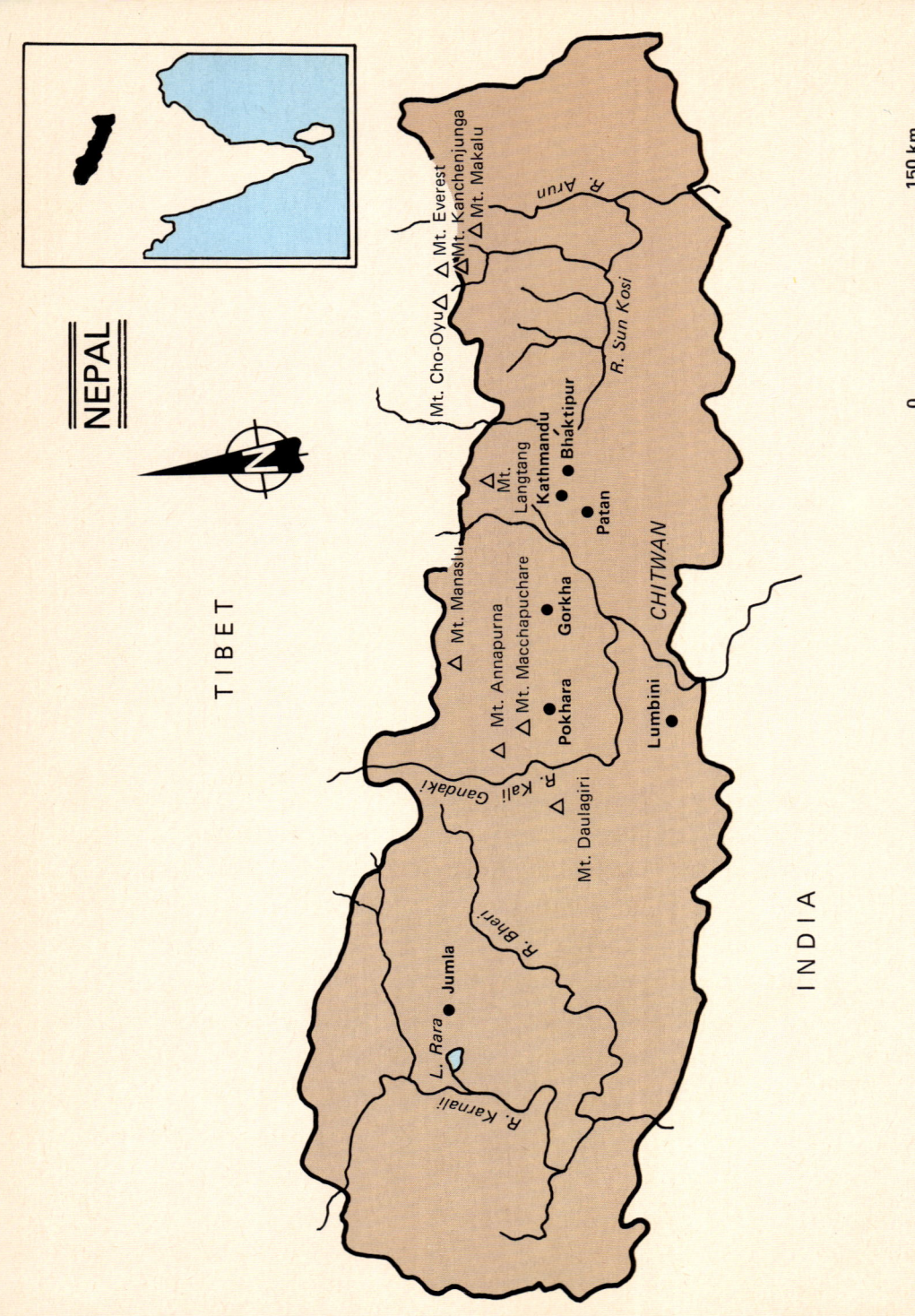

A Himalayan Kingdom

Until the second half of the twentieth century, Nepal was virtually unknown to the rest of the world. It was one of those remote lands forbidden to foreigners. Only in 1951, after King Tribhuvan had put an end to more than a century of political domination by the powerful Rana family, did the world's only Hindu monarchy open its doors to outsiders. Since then, this small nation, one of the world's least developed and most beautiful, has drawn many visitors from the west. They come because they are eager to explore a society so completely different from their own highly industrialized modern civilizations.

Nepal is often described as a "Himalayan kingdom", conjuring up a vision of a tiny country perched in the clouds against a backdrop of snow-clad mountains. The real picture is, in fact, far more interesting and quite as romantic if not so much like a fairy-tale. Although a country of only 141,577 square kilometres (54,000 square miles), Nepal has the greatest altitude range in the world and can boast examples of almost all the climatic zones of the earth—from arctic wastes to hot, tropical jungles. Roughly rectangular in shape—about 800 kilometres (500 miles) in length and up to 240 kilometres (150 miles) in width—Nepal is wedged between two large neighbours: India and China. The country can be divided geographically into five

The Khumbu Glacier, which flows from Mount Everest to Sherpa country

fairly distinctive regions (going north from the Indian border): the Terai, the Siwalik Hills, the Mahabharat Lekh, the Nepal midlands and the Himalayas.

The Terai is a narrow strip of fertile jungle which runs the length of Nepal's border with India. Until recent years the whole area was subject to a most virulent form of malaria which made it almost impossible for people to live there. The only exceptions were those long-established peoples who had built up some resistance to the disease. However, the success of the malarial eradication programme has led to a considerable increase in the local population and to the large-scale clearing of dense jungles.

The Terai is now the most economically productive region in the country, comprising about sixty-five per cent of the cultivable land. It makes a major contribution to the country's earnings each year. One of the results of the development of the area is the decline in the varied and interesting wildlife. However, the government of Nepal is aware of the dangers of extinction which threaten rare species of the Terai. Several wildlife reserves have now been established as well as the Chitwan National Park, where it is possible to go on organized tours, either on foot or riding on an elephant. Tiger, leopard, bear, rhinoceros, wild water-buffalo and several species of deer are some of the animals that live in the Terai. Crocodiles and other more unusual water creatures, including the freshwater Gangetic dolphin (which has almost vanished from the Ganges itself) can be found in its rivers.

North of the Terai are the Siwalik Hills, the southernmost reach of the Himalayas. In some places, they come right down to the Indian border. In others, they are joined to the Mahabharat Lekh, another range of hills which form the third geographic zone of the country. These neighbouring regions are sparsely populated because of the thick forests and the scarcity of water. The Siwaliks are virtually uninhabited, but some large settlements can be found at the lower altitudes of the Mahabharat Lekh, where there are summits which rise to about 2,700 metres (9,000 feet). The river gorges and valleys are very beautiful but because of the overwhelming presence of the

Herding goats near the town of Pokhara. The Himalayan mountain of Macchapuchare can be seen in the background

Himalayas at close quarters, people show comparatively little interest in these lesser regions.

The Nepal midlands, which are protected from the harsh cold and winds of the Tibetan plateau by the Himalayas and from the searing heat of the Indian plains by the Mahabharat Lekh, enjoy a generally pleasant climate. The region is the most densely populated in the whole country and is divided by transverse rivers into a number of wide valleys. The principal valley is that of Kathmandu where the capital is situated. It offers the rich mosaic of Hindu and Buddhist arts and cultures that give Nepalese society its unique, colourful character. Hinduism and Buddhism are two religions which were born in India thousands of years ago and which, over the centuries, have developed as major world civilizations.

To the west of Kathmandu is the valley of Pokhara which attracts many visitors because of its beautiful lakes and the spectacular views of the mountains that rise up from the relatively low valley floor—880 metres (2,900 feet) above sea-level—to peaks as high as 7,000 metres (23,000 feet).

Most of the midland soil is fertile and there is intensive cultivation of a variety of food crops, such as rice, wheat and maize. In the seventeenth and eighteenth centuries, small mining ventures and metal works developed in the valleys. But, as their

Workers in a ricefield in the midlands, one of Nepal's most fertile areas, where a variety of food crops are grown

main product was weapons, these minor industries died out when the import of arms from Britain began in the nineteenth century.

The largest of Nepal's geographical divisions and, of course, the most famous is the Himalayas. This region covers not just the actual mountain range but the foothills, the large valleys (known as the Inner Himalayas) that lie behind the main peaks, and the Tibetan Marginal Mountains which are, in fact, the southern edge of the Tibetan plateau. The presence of the highest peaks in the world, their difficulty of access, the wealth of flora and fauna and the sheer natural beauty of it all make this youngest of mountain ranges also the most fascinating, shrouded in all kinds of myths and mystery.

The Himalayas stretch from Afghanistan in the west to Burma in the east. Some of the most famous summits are accessible from Nepal. Everest, the highest mountain in the world at 8,484 metres (29,028 feet), was first conquered by man in 1953, but it regularly continues to attract aspiring climbers of different nationalities. There are also other mountains in the Nepal Himalayas which can rival Everest in beauty and majesty if not in height: Kanchenjunga, Makalu, Cho-Oyu, Daulagiri, Annapurna, Manaslu and the breathtakingly lovely Macchapuchare, are some of the better known ones. For the peoples of Nepal as well as for other Hindus and Buddhists, the Himalayas are not just high elevations which must be climbed to prove man's ability to dominate nature, they are divine mountains sacred to the gods. Their feelings of reverence

The snow-clad peak of Manaslu, with a Buddhist hermitage in the foreground

and awe are not unmixed with fear, for the geological movements that accompany the still continuing (but very slight) growth of the Himalayas result in earthquakes, landslides and floods which can be extremely destructive.

It might be expected that the rivers would flow north or south on either side of the world's highest mountain range. But in this, as in many other aspects, the Himalayas are unique. The waters divide further north on the Tibetan plateau and, when they eventually turn south, they force their way through the

A deep river gorge north of Gorkha in central Nepal

mountains, creating deep river gorges. The valley of the Kali Gandaki river in central Nepal is said to be the deepest gorge in the world, forming the divide between Annapurna and Daulagiri, both of which tower above 7,925 metres (26,000 feet).

Going north from the Nepal midlands into the foothills of the Himalayas and up towards the mountains and high valleys is a journey through several climatic zones. The variations are caused not just by the changes in altitude but also by the fact that the mountains affect the passage of the monsoon winds. It is these winds which bring the seasonal rains that play such an important role in the life of southern Asia. The winds forced up the southern and central slopes of the Himalayas drop their load of water and make those regions very wet, while the upper slopes get much less rain and the high valleys behind the mountain barriers are almost desert.

The Himalayas are a naturalist's paradise with a great range of plant-, bird- and animal-life. The rhododendron, which is Nepal's national flower, can be found in most parts of the country from the hot southern regions to the high forests. At higher levels walnuts, camellias, magnolias and, still further up, birch, orchids and conifers, join the parade of rich plant-life that adorns the Himalayan slopes. Above the tree-line are alpine meadows with their glorious spring and summer carpets of primulas, irises, gentians, fritillaries and other wild flowers.

The bird population decreases as the low valleys give way to the mountains but there is still a considerable selection which includes the Himalayan griffon vulture, golden eagle, pheasant, snow pigeon and snow partridge. The animals of the Himalayas are no less interesting than the big game of the Terai: bear, wild boar, langur monkeys and red pandas live in the lower altitudes. Higher up there are musk deer, blue sheep, goat antelope, snow leopard and, of course, the yak which is closely associated with all the Himalayan countries. This is by no means an exhaustive list of all the species that can be found. Among

Tibetan snowcocks—an unusual species of bird found in the Himalayas

them we should perhaps include the yeti, or Abominable Snowman—a strange creature like an ape-man, surrounded by legend and speculation, whose existence or non-existence has not yet been proved conclusively. The yeti is still one of the mysteries that make the Himalayas such a storehouse of wonders.

The World's Only Hindu Monarchy

Until fairly recent times the name Nepal was applied only to the Kathmandu valley. The history of Nepal, therefore, is largely the history of the valley. Mention of the country that is now Nepal can be found in ancient Indian literature. It is also the acknowledged birthplace of the Lord Buddha, who lived over 2,500 years ago. However, there is not enough historical material to give us a clear view of the past until about the fourth century A.D.

This was the period when Nepal fell under the rule of the Lichhavi kings who came from northern India. Under these kings there developed strong ties between Nepal and her southern neighbour: there was much Indian influence on Nepalese art and culture, and Sanskrit (the ancient language of northern India) was used at the court of the Lichhavis. The kings were Buddhists as well as Hindus and it was during their dynasty that the sacred and most famous Buddhist monument in Nepal—Swayambunath—was built. Apart from relations with India, Nepal under the Lichhavis also had important links with her northern neighbour Tibet, especially in the sphere of trade. Tibet was very powerful in the sixth and seventh centuries and it is thought by some historians that it might even have exercised political domination over Nepal for some time.

The power of the Lichhavi kings seems to have died out in the ninth century. Not much is known about Nepalese history between the late ninth century and the beginning of the thirteenth century. It was probably a time of trouble and frequent changes, causing the country to be divided into many small kingdoms. During this period the Muslims conquered northern India, but although they extended their military expeditions to the Kathmandu valley they did not remain in Nepal, which was left to its own troubles.

By the beginning of the thirteenth century, however, the Kathmandu valley again became settled enough to produce a steady line of monarchs, who came to be known as the Malla

Part of Swayambunath, the most famous Buddhist monument in Nepal, built in the time of the Lichhavi kings

A statue of King Bhupatindra Malla in the city of Bhaktipur. The archway in the background is known as the Golden Gate and is sometimes described as the finest piece of art in Nepal

kings. The Mallas, like the Lichhavis, were of Indian origin. Under their rule, Hindu practices became more firmly established. The period of Malla rule was the time when Muslim power was taking root in India, forcing many Hindus and Buddhists to flee north to Nepal. Perhaps because of the difficulties of moving and fighting in a mountainous country with a southern border of thick, unhealthy jungle, or perhaps because they were too busy with their conquests in India, the Muslims left Nepal alone after a single raid in the fourteenth century.

However, because of trade and other links with India, a certain amount of Muslim cultural influence came to the Kathmandu valley, particularly at the court of the Malla kings. But, as far as religion was concerned, the Mallas remained unshaken in their Hindu faith and under them Buddhism became weakened and both Hindu social customs and religious practices came to dominate Nepalese life. At the beginning of the thirteenth century Buddhism in Nepal had been strong enough for its influence to reach Tibet. By the sixteenth century, Tibet itself had become a stronghold of Buddhism while Nepal was almost completely overwhelmed by Hinduism.

The early stage of Malla rule had brought some stability, but there were too many small independent states all around the Kathmandu valley for the country to be united and at peace for long. There were many quarrels among the Mallas themselves; in fact, their divisions were so great that by the early seventeenth century the Kathmandu valley had broken up into three separate kingdoms, all under Malla kings. Since the whole valley is about the size of a large metropolis, these little kingdoms were hardly more than city-states. The capitals of these tiny kingdoms were Kathmandu city, Patan and Bhaktipur. The exact size of each state kept changing all the time, as the kings made war on each other and seized whatever territory they could. Other states surrounding the Kathmandu valley were drawn into the quarrels of the Malla kings, who were always seeking outside support for their internal feuds. This caused the hill states to the west of the Kathmandu valley to play an increasing role in the politics of the valley.

One of these states was Gorkha, whose kings (like many of the ruling families in Nepal) claimed to be descended from the Rajputs—a militant clan from northern India. The many occasions on which the kings of Gorkha were asked to give help to one Malla kingdom or another during the seventeenth and early eighteenth centuries led them to become interested in conquering the Kathmandu valley, which controlled the important trade route between India and Tibet. The Gorkha kings began by carrying out a gradual conquest of the territory surrounding the valley. They then tried to take over the valley itself, but their first attempts were not successful. Finally, in 1768-9, King Prithvi Narayan Shah seized the opportunity presented by the disunity, constant fighting and treachery among the three kingdoms to put an end to Malla rule and establish his power over the whole valley.

Prithvi Narayan Shah and his descendants set up their capital in Kathmandu city and expanded their kingdom steadily, bringing more and more of the surrounding hill states and tribal groups under their rule. Sometimes they used military force and sometimes they made treaties, and so Nepal gradually began to acquire the shape it has today. The Gorkha kings were ambitious and their desire to increase the area over which they wielded their power naturally led to clashes with their

A modern view of Kathmandu city. It was here that Prithvi Narayan Shah and his descendants set up their capital in the late eighteenth century

neighbours. Their military invasions of Tibet provoked the Chinese, who counter-attacked on the side of the Tibetans. In 1792, the Nepalese were defeated by the Chinese and this put an end to any ideas they might have had of expanding their kingdom to the north.

They then turned their attention to the south. The second half of the eighteenth century was a time when the British East India Company was establishing its rule over India. In 1767, one of the Malla kings asked for the Company's help against

Prithvi Narayan Shah. The difficulties of crossing the Terai jungles during the heavy rains of the monsoon season had caused the Company troops to turn back, but the British continued to keep an anxious eye on Nepal. The rising power of the Gorkha kings at Kathmandu increased their anxiety, especially after the Nepalese aggression in Tibet. In 1814, war broke out between Nepal and the East India Company as a result of repeated military excursions by the Nepalese into Indian territory.

The war finally came to an end in 1816 when the military successes of the Company troops, who almost got to the point of invading the Kathmandu valley, led to the Nepalese admitting defeat and agreeing to sign a treaty. Under this treaty they handed over some of their southern territory to British India, establishing a border which has remained almost unchanged to the present day.

The British had been so impressed by the quality of the troops of the Gorkha kings that, under the same treaty, they made arrangements for Nepalese soldiers to serve in their armies in India. This was the beginning of a long military association which still continues to this day. The great majority of Nepalese who serve in the British and Indian armies are, in fact, recruited not from among the people of Gorkha (who are known as "Gorkhalis") but rather from other racial groups in Nepal. However, it is as "Gurkhas" that they have become famous throughout the world for their courage and fighting skill.

The Shah dynasty brought about a stronger, more unified state. However, during the nineteenth century, many divisions appeared within the ruling family. A number of the kings came to the throne while still minors and this led to a decline in the powers of the monarch; ministers became very strong and often exercised more influence than the king. Rivalry for powerful positions increased, as did quarrels among the ruling classes. And political murder became a common way of settling disagreements. The distrust and hatred among the groups surrounding the royal court and the readiness with which violence was used to resolve quarrels finally led, in the 1840s, to the supreme power passing from the hands of the Shah kings into those of a line of hereditary prime ministers.

A nobleman called Jung Bahadur was asked by the queen of King Rajendra Bikram Shah to support her against her enemies. Jung Bahadur acceded to the queen's request and, in 1846, his troops massacred large numbers of Nepal's noblemen and political and military leaders at a court ceremony. Jung Bahadur then became prime minister. But, soon afterwards, he fell out with the queen who, together with the king, fled to India. This left the prime minister as the most powerful figure in the country. He then placed a king of his own choice on the throne.

This was the beginning of more than a hundred years' rule by members of Jung Bahadur's family, who came to be known as "Ranas" after a title conferred on him by the king in 1858. The Shah monarchs continued to sit on the throne but they had no real power and often seemed like prisoners in their own palaces.

Jung Bahadur Rana and his successors kept Nepal closed to the outside world, cutting the country off from new developments which began to take place elsewhere during the late nineteenth century and early twentieth century. It has therefore been said that the Ranas made Nepal a backward, isolated nation. Nevertheless, they did bring about certain changes aimed at creating a more modern society. They put a stop to slavery and to the practice of widows burning themselves to death on their husband's funeral pyres (in accordance with Hindu custom). Jung Bahadur also tried to create a uniform system of law and government for the whole country; and this work was carried on by some of his abler successors.

A Rana family group in their heyday

Like the Shah kings, the Ranas wanted Nepal united under a strong government at Kathmandu. However, they were not interested in sharing power with those outside their own family. In addition, there was little trust and unity within the family. Just as the divisions among the royal circle had led to the Ranas usurping the real power from the Shah kings, the constant quarrels within the Rana family were to lead to their own downfall and the subsequent restoration of the powers of the monarch.

Opposition to the Rana monopoly of political power in Nepal began to appear in the 1920s. Nepalese who had lived or been educated abroad (and those who had become aware of the activities of the Indian nationalists who were opposing British rule in India) became politically conscious and eager to challenge the power of the Ranas. The end of the Second World War brought about further developments which were unfavourable to the rule of the hereditary prime ministers. India became independent, and the removal of the British from the country meant the removal of the strong support which the Ranas had enjoyed since the days of Jung Bahadur. (He had been on good terms with Britain and had even been to London on a state visit.) The Indians who took over the government of their own country had closer ties with the political opponents of the Ranas, who were too divided among themselves to be able to stand firm against their enemies. The dissatisfaction among the Nepalese with their system of government was probably also increased by the new ideas and attitudes brought back by the hundreds of thousands of Gurkhas returning from the war. The Ranas tried to win the support of India. But, although a treaty was signed in 1950, in the same year the Indian government helped King Tribhuvan to escape from Nepal, where he had lived totally under the power and at the mercy of the Ranas.

Once outside his own country, the king became an important element in the forces opposing Rana rule. The Ranas tried to hold out, but the tide was too strong against them. In 1951, the Indian government helped to bring about an agreement which brought King Tribhuvan and many anti-Rana politicians back to Nepal. The Rana prime minister kept his post, but his powers were greatly reduced. The days of the political domination by Jung Bahadur's family were brought to an end. Nepal was once again a monarchy in fact as well as in name.

Entering the Modern World

The restoration of the king's powers in 1951 brought about many changes in Nepal. The country opened its doors to the rest of the world and began to take its place among the nations of the twentieth century. However, it was not easy to introduce new ideas and practices quickly to a country which had been isolated for more than a hundred years. The opponents of the Rana regime who had come back with King Tribhuvan wanted Nepal to be run as a democratic country with an elected government. But, like politicians everywhere, they were divided in their aims and methods. As a result, the early years of the restored monarchy were a time for trying to find a system of government which was both efficient and acceptable to the country.

King Tribhuvan lived only until 1955. He was succeeded by his son Mahendra. The political parties had grown strong under Tribhuvan and important government positions were held by the party leaders. In 1959, elections were held and Nepal had its first elected government. But in 1960 King Mahendra dissolved parliament, had many politicians arrested and took the government of the country into his own hands. It is not clear whether the king's decision to turn back the democratic process was taken because he felt that the system was not suitable to the country or because he wanted a more active and influential role for the monarch. It must not, however, be thought that Nepal was turned entirely into a dictatorship where the voice of the people was never heard. Mahendra used a system of village councils (*panchayats*) to give the people a say in the running of their country.

Under this system, councils in villages and towns elected representatives to district councils. These, in turn, elected members of the zone councils, and so on like a pyramid—as far as the National Panchayat in Kathmandu. The National Panchayat can have discussions and make proposals relating to the laws of the land. Although it is up to the king to decide whether or not he will accept the suggestions of the Panchayat,

The National Panchayat (parliament) building in Kathmandu

its opinions are thought to have a certain amount of influence on the government.

Mahendra died in 1972 and was succeeded by his son Birendra, who had been educated in England, the United States and Japan. The new king continued with a system of government based on *panchayats*, and political parties remained illegal as they had been under his father. However, it is widely believed that he wishes to bring about changes in the political system to make it better suited to a developing nation. King Birendra's great concern is for the social and economic development of his country, which is still one of the poorest in the world.

There are many problems facing a small, landlocked state which tries to make the change from a backward, almost medieval society to modern, twentieth-century nationhood. Nepal's economy is still largely based on agriculture, with less than five per cent of the working population engaged in industry. The country has some mineral resources, but these appear to be fairly limited. One of the biggest problems is that the capacity of the land to produce food crops is poor in the midlands and the northern hill areas, although great efforts are being made to improve the situation. Under the Ranas many farmers had to work very hard only to hand over most of the fruit of their labours to powerful landlords. There was thus little interest in trying to improve the quality of the land and its produce. But, since new laws have been brought in to enable the farmers to keep a fairer share of their produce, there have been efforts

Women cleaning rice in a small village in northern Nepal. Although Nepal's economy is largely based on agriculture, modern farming methods are not yet widespread

towards increasing the yield of the land. Modern scientific knowledge and methods have also been playing an important part in making agriculture more efficient and productive.

Nepal shares with other poor nations the need to develop in three important areas: health, education and communications. Large numbers of Nepalese babies die during the first years of their lives, and many people suffer from diseases such as smallpox and cholera which have almost been wiped out in the more developed countries. There are not enough hospitals or trained medical staff. Poor Nepalese in villages far from a doctor sometimes have to live for years with illnesses which could be cured quite easily with the right treatment. Much disease is

A man with a goitre caused by the lack of iodine in the local diet

caused and spread by the unhealthy conditions in which many people live; so to improve health there is also a need for education.

There are not many schools in Nepal and, even where there are schools, it is not easy to get the local children to come regularly. The rate of literacy in Nepal is low, about twenty-five per cent for men and boys and five per cent for girls and women. A central problem is finding enough money to train teachers and build schools. Even when there are teachers available, there are not many who wish to work in the villages and remote areas. The construction of schools is particularly time-consuming and expensive in Nepal because of the difficulties of transport and communications.

A country as mountainous as Nepal faces many problems when it comes to building roads, which require great engineering skill. A network of roads linking remote parts of the country to the more developed areas is under construction, but progress is not very quick. However, there are highways from India to Kathmandu and one from Kathmandu to Lhasa in Tibet. This makes a journey from India all the way to Beijing (the capital of China) by way of Nepal and Tibet an exciting possibility.

Nepal is a small country and, as already mentioned, the lack of sufficient medical care causes many babies to die shortly after birth. In spite of this, the population is increasing very rapidly indeed. It is one of the big concerns of government to try and keep it under control. Over-population is not a new problem

A game of volley-ball, played at 3,660 metres (12,000 feet) above sea-level in the Himalayas

in Nepal; it is many decades since it first became necessary for Nepalese to go out of their country to find work in neighbouring states. Large numbers of foreign labourers are generally not welcome and in recent years it has become increasingly difficult for Nepalese to find work abroad. Efficient family planning has therefore become one of the main aims of those working for the greater development of Nepal.

Over-population and the low capacity of the land to produce food has led to another of the country's major problems. Large portions of the forests that cover the mountain slopes have been cut down to increase the area of land where crops can be grown and to provide wood for fuel. One of the worst effects of destroying forests is that the ground becomes exposed to rain and wind and gradually wears away. Not only does this result in a poorer quality soil, the loosened earth (which can cause landslides) eventually settles down in the river-beds. This reduces the capacity of the rivers to contain their waters and floods become more frequent, particularly down in the plains. A programme for preserving the remaining forests and replanting those which have been thinned down or even completely destroyed is now one of Nepal's important projects.

Nepal has been greatly helped in its efforts towards modernization by the aid of richer nations, in particular by India and China. As a small country which could not hope to defend itself militarily against either of its two powerful neighbours, Nepal has the task of protecting its independence by taking care to be on good terms with both. In this, as in its other efforts

Workers' huts on the site of a hydro-electricity project near Pokhara. The Chinese are providing technical assistance on this

towards gaining a place among the nations of the twentieth century, Nepal can be said to have achieved a fair amount of success in spite of its many problems.

Worshipping the Gods

In Nepal, religion is very much a part of people's everyday life. The long centuries during which Hinduism and Buddhism have existed side by side have given both religions a particularly Nepalese stamp.

Hinduism is very difficult to define and has been described as both a social system and a religion. The term "Hindu" is simply a Persian word meaning "Indian", and Hinduism is in fact the name for the way of life and the religious beliefs and practices which developed in India over many centuries before the beginning of the Christian era. It is a mixture of the customs and religious beliefs of the Aryans who invaded India between 4000 and 1000 B.C. and those of the original inhabitants of the land they conquered. Although there are many Hindu gods, Hinduism is not a religion which requires absolute belief in one particular god or group of gods, and it covers a large range of ideas and types of worship. However, a necessary condition of being a Hindu is acceptance of the caste system, which divides people according to the class and group into which they are born. There are numerous castes and sub-castes but the four major ones are the Brahmins (priests), Kshatriyas (warriors, including kings and nobles), Vaishyas (most ordinary people who are neither priests nor warriors) and Sudras (the "untouchables").

An image of the Hindu god Shiva the Destroyer. Hinduism and Buddhism have long existed side by side in Nepal and the intermingling has given Nepalese religion its special character

Strict Hindus are very careful to keep the caste laws and will have very few social dealings with members of different castes. Even today, with governments promoting modern attitudes about the equality of all and trying to break down the barriers between different social groups, caste feelings are still strong among many Hindus.

Buddhism developed much later than Hinduism. It is a religion based on the teachings of a great man who lived about 560 B.C. to 480 B.C. His name was Siddhartha and he was the son of the king of a small state in northern India. His birthplace is at Lumbini in southern Nepal. Siddhartha gave up his princely life to search for a way which would help to free all beings from the sufferings that come with existence. After several years of study and deep thinking on the nature and cause of suffering, he came to understand it. He then went around the countryside teaching people how best they might avoid suffering by learning to control their own thoughts and desires. Because he had achieved the great wisdom which enabled him to free himself and all those who followed his teachings from the mistaken ideas and false beliefs that lead to suffering, he came to be known as the Buddha, or Enlightened One.

The Lord Buddha was born a Hindu but, although he did not reject the religion of his fathers, he did not hold with the social divisions of the caste system. His teachings were based on loving kindness towards all beings. Because of this and other differences between the Hindus and the followers of the Lord Buddha, Buddhism came to be thought of as a separate religion.

Both Hinduism and Buddhism came to Nepal from India, but while Buddhism all but died out in the land of its origin, it continued to exist in Nepal, side by side with Hinduism. However, many Hindu ideas and practices have crept into the Buddhism of Nepal, the most noticeable of which is the caste system. Nepalese Buddhists are divided into castes along Hindu

Buddhist prayer wheels. These contain pieces of paper on which prayers are written. People turn the wheels clockwise to acquire merit

lines, in spite of the teachings of the Lord Buddha against such divisions. Further, both Nepalese Hinduism and Buddhism have been greatly influenced by ideas and religious practices which are full of hidden meanings and mysterious rituals based on a body of writings known as the Tantras.

The Nepalese respect each other's religious beliefs and practices. Throughout their history there has been goodwill and understanding between the Hindus and the Buddhists. Some of the kings did try to spread Hindu social customs in the country, but they also treated the Buddhists well and often gave their support and encouragement to both religions alike. It is quite usual to find Buddhist sacred images in Hindu religious buildings as well as the other way round. Whether a Nepalese calls himself a Buddhist or a Hindu usually depends on whether the family priest is Buddhist or Hindu rather than on how and where they worship.

In a country where religion plays such an important part, it is not surprising to find that there are many festivals connected with worship in some form or other. In the Kathmandu valley there is a festival every month, except during June and July, when the people are busy with rice transplanting. Many of the

A Hindu chanting morning prayers in Kathmandu

festivals are devoted to Hindu gods and goddesses; others celebrate important Buddhist religious days; still others honour ancestors, parents and brothers. There are even festivals not just for the cow, which is considered holy by the Hindus, but also for such humble animals as the dog and the frog. The dates of all the festivals are decided according to the lunar calendar. Among the most important of Nepal's colourful and interesting festivals are Rato Machhendranath Rath Jatra, Indra Jatra, Dasain or Durga Puja, Tihar or Divali, Bala Chaturdasi and Holi.

Machhendranath is one of those gods worshipped by both Hindus and Buddhists in Nepal. He is seen by many as the patron deity of the Kathmandu valley, and farmers worship him as the god who gives agricultural prosperity. The festival of Rato (red) Machhendranath is celebrated in April when the image of the god is taken from his temple in Patan and carried in a huge chariot with a tall spire, which is dragged along the streets by hundreds of people. The procession makes stops at several places where offerings are made to Machhendranath and animals are sacrificed to keep the angry god Bhairab, who forms the wheels of the chariot, from taking human life. It is a colourful festival and there is much excitement and noise as the people jostle to accompany the god who is being taken to a temple in Bunga village in the Kathmandu valley, where he stays for several months of the year.

Indra Jatra takes place in September and is celebrated in memory of a time when the people of the Kathmandu valley

The chariot procession of the Living Goddess of Kathmandu, which forms the highlight of the festival of Indra Jatra. The young girl who has been chosen as the Living Goddess, or Kumari, can be seen in the centre of the picture

were supposed to have taken the god Indra prisoner, not knowing his true identity. The festival begins with the raising of Indra's flag before the old palace at Hanuman Dhoka in Kathmandu. This is followed by four days of ceremonies, dances and the worship of those religious images which are unveiled only during this festival. Perhaps the most exciting part of Indra Jatra is the chariot procession of the Living Goddess of Kathmandu.

The Living Goddess (or Kumari, as she is called) is a young girl who is worshipped as a form of the goddess Durga. The custom of selecting a young girl to be a Living Goddess is one of the more interesting features of religion in Nepal. There are a number of Kumaris in the country, with about eleven in the Kathmandu valley alone. The most important one is the State Kumari, who lives in Kathmandu city. Normally, a Kumari is chosen (while still a child of three or four) from the Buddhist Shakya caste of the Newaris. She is supposed to be without physical blemishes and to possess special signs showing her to be the goddess in the form of a human girl, and she must pass certain tests put to her by the committee responsible for selecting the Kumaris. Once chosen, the State Kumari lives in a Buddhist religious building at Durbar Square in Kathmandu and is worshipped as the Living Goddess until puberty. The Kumari

Selling flowers for the Dasain festival

ceases to be divine if she sheds blood. So, if she so much as cuts her little finger and bleeding takes place before puberty, she can no longer be regarded as the Living Goddess. When one Kumari retires, another is immediately chosen to take her place. It is considered part of the duties of the State Kumari to advise and guide the monarch and the people. During Indra Jatra she is drawn in a towering chariot to the old palace to give her blessings to the king.

Dasain is the most important Nepalese festival, celebrated throughout the country for a fortnight in October or late September, during which little is done that is not connected with

Part of the Dasain festivities, which celebrate the victory of good over evil

the festivities devoted to the victory of good over evil. Dasain means "tenth", for the celebrations which are most intense in the first nine days lead to the Tenth Day of Victory. The festival is also known as Durga Puja, as it is a time for special worship of the goddess Durga—the great Mother Goddess who freed the people from the miseries caused by evil forces.

Among the Hindu deities, there are the gentle ones who only accept offerings of "pure" foods such as fruit and milk products, while there are others for whom blood sacrifices are considered suitable. Deities can have more than one form and different forms may be worshipped in different ways. The Goddess Durga is one of the frightening forms of the wife of Shiva, one of the most important and powerful, sometimes considered *the* most powerful, of the Hindu gods. The worship of this goddess in the terrifying form in which she destroyed the forces of evil involves much blood sacrifice. During Dasain many animals are slaughtered in religious rites to honour and please the goddess. Apart from the sacrifices performed by private individuals, there are also those organized by the government and the army. In the past there used to be human sacrifices to Durga. This is, of course, illegal now although people whisper that it still goes on in some places.

The tenth day celebrates not just the victory of Durga over an evil demon called Mahisasura, but also the victory of Rama (a great hero king of Hindu mythology) over another demon, Ravana. On this day Nepalese visit their elders and superiors to whom they pay their respects and from whom they receive

Nepalese children with the *tika* mark of red paste on their foreheads. This is a mark of blessing which the Nepalese receive from their elders and superiors on the tenth day of the Dasain Festival

blessings in the form of the *tika* mark of red paste on the forehead.

Dasain is closely followed by another festival called Divali or Tihar, when for five nights lamps are lit to worship Laxmi, goddess of wealth. It is also known as the Five Days of Yama, god of the dead. And on different days of the festival, Yama's messenger—the crow—and his gate-keeper—the dog—are honoured. Tihar is traditionally a time for gambling, for Laxmi is said to frown on money exchanging hands in any other way during her festival. Since gambling was made illegal in 1950, it is now done only in private.

Bala Chaturdasi is a time when ceremonies for the dead are performed by living relatives at the temple of Pashupatinath, the most holy of Hindu shrines in Nepal. It takes place at the end of November or early December when people not just from the Kathmandu valley but even from as far away as India come to Pashupatinath to fast, pray for the dead, and light lamps and torches which they cast into the river. They also take part in a barefoot pilgrimage around the temple hill, scattering grain on holy stones and images along the route.

Holi takes place in March. It is an ancient Hindu festival

The golden-roofed temple of Pashupatinath, the most holy Hindu shrine in Nepal

when people are allowed to throw bright pink powder and coloured water on each other and on cows and animals for eight days, although nowadays most of the play is restricted to one day. Nobody is supposed to get angry during Holi, so a certain amount of liberty is taken and sometimes tempers *are* lost. But, on the whole, it is a happy festival.

There are many other Nepalese festivals, full of interest and colourful details. To understand and appreciate them it is necessary to have some idea of the religious beliefs behind the celebrations which may seem meaningless or even unpleasant (as in the case of the animal sacrifices), unless one knows something of the reasons why certain things are done. However, it must also be remembered that the Nepalese are a fun-loving, cheerful people. There is no doubt that their festivals are in large part meant to be enjoyed by those who celebrate them as well as by those who are merely observers.

A Medley of Peoples

Nepal is a land of many racial groups and tribes. They can be roughly divided between the Tibeto-Nepalese and the Indo-Nepalese. The first are related to the Chinese and Mongolians to the north and speak Tibeto-Burman languages. The second are related to the Indians of the south and they use Indo-Aryan languages.

In the past, the different racial groups kept very separate from each other; apart from those who actually lived in the Kathmandu valley, they did not think of themselves as belonging to Nepal at all. However, since Nepalese governments have started promoting the idea of a united country, and since modern life and communications have made it not only possible but sometimes necessary for the different peoples to have dealings with each other, the divisions between the racial groups are not as wide as they used to be. There are still differences in attitudes and customs, but the people of Nepal are now beginning to think of themselves not just as separate races but also as belonging to the same nation.

It is convenient when discussing the peoples of Nepal to list them according to the area in which they are to be found—the Terai in the south, the midlands and the higher altitudes to the north. The group most widely distributed throughout the country is that of the high-caste Hindus who came from northern India. These Brahmins and Chhetris (Kshatriyas, some of whom intermarried with local peoples and formed sub-castes) were traditionally the richest and most influential, including among them big landowners.

The Newars are the people considered to be the original inhabitants of the Kathmandu valley. The great majority of them still live there. There are Mongolian as well as Mediterranean physical types among them and they speak Newari (a Tibeto-Burman language) as well as Nepali which is Indo-Aryan. From this it seems likely that they have been in the Kathmandu valley since very ancient times and, in the course of the centuries, mixed both with peoples coming from the north and those from the south.

There are both Buddhists and Hindus among them, but there is not always a very clear division between the religious practices of the two groups, most of whom seem to have taken elements from both religions. However, Hindu influence may be said to be stronger overall, especially as the caste system which the Lord Buddha did not accept is observed quite strictly among Newari Buddhists. Many of the important festivals already mentioned, such as Indra Jatra, are Newari. And, in the Kathmandu valley, there are numerous examples of Newar art and architecture. The Newars have been particularly fine artisans and traders since way back in history. Many of them went to live and practise their crafts in Tibet as long ago as the seventh century. Today, Newars still make up large numbers

A street seller in Kathmandu city. The original inhabitants of the Kathmandu valley were the Newars, and many Newars still live there

of the merchants and shopkeepers in the Kathmandu valley. They also occupy many positions in government departments.

Another interesting group of people in the Nepal midlands are the Rai and the Limbu, who are together classed as Kirantis. The Kirantis are a Mongolian-type people speaking Tibeto-Burman languages. It is believed that they came from Tibet to Nepal in ancient times. The Kathmandu valley is traditionally thought to have been ruled by Kirantis before the arrival of the Lichhavis. The Limbu and the Rai live in the easternmost hills of the Nepal midlands and, like the majority of the people in the country, make their living through agriculture. However, nowadays there are numbers of them who work as labourers in the Terai or as Gurkha soldiers in the British and Indian armies.

The largest single racial group in Nepal is that of the Tamangs—a Mongolian-type people believed to have come to Nepal from Tibet, although much later than the Kirantis. Their religious practices still show the signs of their Tibetan origin: they are Buddhists who place great faith and reliance on their spiritual teachers—the lamas—whose role is a basic part of

Women in the Nepal midlands carrying packs of hay for use as winter fodder

A Gurung cowherd with his animals

Tibetan Buddhism. However, they have been in Nepal long enough for them to celebrate certain Hindu festivals. The Tamangs live in the high hills around Kathmandu valley and are becoming quite well known to foreign trekkers, who often hire them as porters.

The Gurungs live in the foothills of the Annapurna and Lamjung Himalayas, right in the very heart of Nepal. Another group of Mongolian stock who came to settle in Nepal many centuries back, they are divided between Hindus and Buddhists, roughly according to whether they live at lower or higher altitudes. There are many Gurungs in Gorkha and they took part in the expeditions of the Shah kings which led to the expansion of the Gorkha kingdom. It is therefore not surprising that, apart from their traditional agriculture and animal husbandry, Gurungs are also to be found serving as Gurkha soldiers outside Nepal.

Some of the other peoples to be found in the Nepal midlands are the Magars, Sunwars, Jirels and Thakalis—all of Mongolian stock, speaking Tibeto-Burman languages. Like the Gurungs, they are mainly agriculturalists who produce just enough for their needs. Magars, Sunwars and Jirels are also recruited as soldiers. The Magars, in fact, form the largest group among Gurkha soldiers serving outside Nepal.

It might be expected that the peoples of the Terai would be Indian in origin and customs. Although this is true of the more recent settlers, the original peoples of the Terai are largely of Tibeto-Burman stock. Among these the Tharus form the largest group. They are peasant farmers who hunt and fish, and they claim to be of Rajput origin. Although they are, on the whole, a Mongolian type, they also have certain non-Mongolian features. So it is possible that they *are* the descendants of Rajput settlers who intermarried with the original inhabitants.

The Danwars, Majhis and Darais are other groups in the Terai who resemble the Tharus physically and who also claim Rajput descent. They depend mainly on farming and fishing. From long years in the jungles, they have developed some resistance to malaria.

The people to be found in the eastern Terai are the Rajbansis (Koches), Bodos, Dhimals and Satars. These groups share the racial features of the Tharus and others, but they have been

Jirel women in the Nepal midlands. The Jirels are of Mongolian stock

much more influenced by India in language as well as in religion. Those of the Koches who became thoroughly Hinduised (in general, the wealthier ones) acquired the caste status of Kshatriyas and became known as Rajbansis. Others became Muslims. Yet others kept their old Koch ways and customs. Among the groups of the eastern Terai, the Satars are considered to be of the same stock as the Santals of Bihar in India. They too are farmers and hunters, like most of the long-established peoples of the Terai, all of whom tend to be shy of strangers.

The people who live along Nepal's northern border are generally referred to by the rest of the Nepalese as Bhotias. The term "Bhotia" means Tibetan. This marks them out as peoples who came to settle in the country long after such groups as the Kirantis and Tamangs. Because of their relatively late arrival from Tibet, their religion, customs and languages are very closely related to those of the Tibetans, and they have not been influenced by Hindu practices and traditions. It must however be remembered that, as Buddhism itself came from Hindu India, there are always certain beliefs and attitudes shared by the two

A Bhotia man in a traditional maroon robe standing in his fields

A woman spinning wool in Solu Khumbu, the Mount Everest region

religions. In the Tibetan type of Buddhism, which is of the Mahayana school, there are also certain practices of a Tantric nature which are similar to the rites of Tantric Hindus.

The Bhotias do not apply this name to themselves and they are, in fact, divided into several distinct groups. Among these, the best-known are the Sherpa people. This is because they live in the area of Mount Everest and came to take part in many mountaineering expeditions as guides and porters. In Nepal today, trekkers and mountaineers use the word "Sherpa" almost as a name for a man who acts as the chief guide, overseer of the porters and general organizer of the details of an expedition. The first groups of Sherpas came to Nepal from Tibet less than five hundred years ago, and they were joined by others who came about three hundred and fifty years later, so their ties with

Tibet are still very strong. Although their language has developed to the extent that they and the Tibetans can no longer understand each other, it has never been forgotten that they are basically one race. Until the Chinese took over Tibet in the 1950s, Sherpas often went over the border for trading expeditions and also sent their monks to be trained in Tibetan monasteries.

Traditionally, the Sherpas were farmers, animal-herders (owning cows, yaks and cross-breeds of the two) and small traders. But, as their land is harsh and not cultivable for long periods of the year, many of them now engage in work connected with trekking and mountaineering. This has brought them many material benefits. At the same time, the influx of foreigners—who are very rich by comparison with them and who introduce new ideas and create new wants—has brought about changes which are not always for the best.

There are a number of other groups of Bhotia peoples, some of whom were organized until fairly modern times in their own little kingdoms or states, such as Mustang and Dolpo. Many of these are even closer to the Tibetans than the Sherpas. Although they are becoming more aware of their political identity as Nepalese, there are no signs yet that their religion and traditions are giving way to Indo-Nepalese influences.

Apart from the various groups of Tibetan origin who have been settled in Nepal long enough for them to be considered Nepalese, there are also those who came in large numbers as refugees from Tibet after that country was invaded by the

A Tibetan refugee camp. Many Tibetans fled to Nepal after the Chinese invaded their country in 1951

Chinese in 1951. Although these recent comers have perhaps not yet come to look upon Nepal as their home, they have not had much difficulty in becoming part of the life of a country which is basically broad-minded and accepts different races and creeds kindly.

The great diversity of peoples in Nepal, with their differences in customs and costumes, makes it difficult to give a description of a "typical" Nepalese. In recent times, the jodhpur-like trousers, western-style jacket and "Gurkha cap" have come to be recognized as the national costume for Nepalese men. But, although an increasing number have come to adopt this style of dress, it cannot be said to be the attire of all Nepalese males.

Many of the racial groups have remained faithful to their various traditional costumes.

The women, even more than the men, keep to their traditional dress. In Nepal can be seen the Indian *sari*, and Tibetan *chuba* and a great array of tribal costumes. But, whatever their dress, the women of Nepal have in common a great liking for jewellery. Some groups favour gold, some silver, some beads and some turquoise and other semi-precious stones. It is indeed a very poor or very unusual Nepalese woman who wears no jewellery at all.

There are considerable differences in the diet of the peoples

Traditional Newari houses in a side street in Bhaktipur. Housing conditions are generally poor in Nepal, with buildings very close together

of Nepal. Rice is the basic food grain for the majority of people; but there are those for whom the main staple is maize and others for whom it is barley or wheat. Few Nepalese outside the high caste Hindu groups are vegetarians, but in such a poor country people can only afford to eat meat sparingly.

Housing conditions in Nepal are generally poor. Even in Kathmandu, the comforts and modern conveniences which people in the west take for granted are still something of a luxury. Often a Newar house, with a facade of beautiful wood carvings, can be as uncomfortable as a mud house in a remote village.

The groups discussed here by no means cover the whole range of peoples to be found in Nepal. But this account gives some idea of the many races and cultures that make up this small but varied and interesting nation.

The Valley of Kathmandu

Kathmandu valley has been described variously by enthusiastic visitors as a Happy Valley, a fairy-tale land, the Florence of Asia, and one big museum where there are more temples and images than men. Perhaps such descriptions are a little exaggerated, but there is certainly much that is fascinating in the major valley of Nepal.

The valley occupies 570 square kilometres (220 square miles) and is situated at about 1,350 metres (4,430 feet) above sea-level, surrounded by hills that rise to about 2,400 metres (nearly 8,000 feet). The surrounding foothills were once heavily forested, but the forests have been cut down gradually as more and more of the valley walls were given over to rice and maize terraces. It is certainly a beautiful place—fertile and brilliant with colour, with the peaks of the Himalayas rising to the north.

The valley is the most developed part of Nepal and the city is at once the biggest, the most important and the one that attracts the greatest number of visitors, especially as it has the only international airport in the country. Kathmandu has much to offer from the point of view of art and architecture too. The three old capitals of the Malla kings—Patan, Bhaktipur and Kathmandu city itself—are full of buildings and monuments

A *stupa* in typical Nepalese style. It is a religious monument containing sacred Buddhist relics. On the base of its tapering tower are painted the "far-seeing eyes of Buddha", looking out to the four points of the compass

which are supreme examples of Newar craftsmanship. They are of great interest as well as being very beautiful.

The most commonly seen among the traditional types of buildings is the brick temple with tiered roofs. This is thought to be a style borrowed from India, although it no longer survives in the country of its origin. Another religious monument is the *stupa* or *chaitan*. In its Nepalese form it is typically a solid dome containing sacred Buddhist relics, topped by a tapering tower in thirteen stages. On the base are painted the beautiful "far-seeing eyes of Buddha" looking out to the four points of

63

the compass. Other buildings of interest and impressive workmanship are the traditional Newari houses and the palaces with elaborate wood-carvings.

The Kathmandu Durbar Square (*durbar* means "royal court"), where the old palace of the city stands, packs a number of historic buildings and monuments into a small area. The palace itself is called Hanuman Dhoka, after the Hindu monkey-god Hanuman, whose statue can be seen at the gate. Hanuman Dhoka was built in the seventeenth century by one of the Malla kings. The Shah kings lived in it until the nineteenth century. The palace has been renovated many times since it was first

A lion statue guarding the entrance to the old royal palace in Kathmandu city

built. In recent years the United Nations Educational and Scientific Organization (UNESCO) has undertaken the work of repairing and restoring some of the main buildings.

There are a number of courtyards in Hanuman Dhoka. The present king of Nepal, who now lives in a more modern and no doubt more comfortable if less beautiful and interesting palace, was crowned in the main courtyard in 1975.

Among the other buildings of historical, religious and artistic interest in the area of the Durbar Square are the Taleju Temple, the Maju Deval, the Kumari Chowk and Kasthamandap. Taleju was the family deity of the Malla kings, and the temple (which was built in the sixteenth century) is a beautiful golden building where non-Hindus are not allowed to enter. The Maju Deval, is another temple with a three-tiered roof, a platform in nine stages and some interesting wood-carvings. The Kumari Chowk, which is the official residence of the Living Goddess of Kathmandu, is a three-storey building with an intricately carved wooden frontage. More examples of the masterly wood-carving of the Newaris can be seen in the courtyard. Foreigners are allowed to enter here, although only Buddhists and Hindus may go beyond into the building itself.

Many tourists and visitors linger around the place hoping to get a glimpse of the Living Goddess but no one is allowed to photograph her in her house. Kasthamandap is a large house supposed to have been constructed from the wood of a single tree. It was built in the seventeenth century as a *sattal,* a kind of temple rest-house. The neighbourhood and the city gradually

The stone image of the Kalo (Black) Bhairab, near Durbar Square in Kathmandu. It is believed that those who tell a lie before the statue die immediately

came to be known by the name of this building, which was large and imposing by traditional Newari standards. Thus, the city that used to be called Kantipur became Kasthamandap, later corrupted to Kathmandu.

Besides temples and palaces, there are a number of statues and images of religious importance and artistic interest around Durbar Square. Among them, the best-known are the Kalo Bhairab and the Sweta Bhairab. Bhairab is the god Shiva in his terrible form. He is worshipped so widely in Nepal that it is estimated there are about five million images of him in the country. The Kalo (Black) Bhairab near Durbar Square is carved from stone and is considered so powerful that it is believed those who tell a lie in its presence die immediately. In the past, criminals were brought before the image and examined to find out whether or not they were telling the truth. Behind the Black Bhairab is the White (Sweta) Bhairab, a huge carved head of the god which is protected by a lattice-work gate, removed only once a year, during Indra Jatra.

Kathmandu city is situated near the middle of the valley, at the junction of two rivers sacred to the Hindus—the Bagmati and the Vishnumati. Across the Bagmati to the south is another old capital. This is Patan, also known as Lalitpur, "City of

The golden door of the royal palace in Patan

Beauty". Among the three capitals of the Malla kings, Patan is considered the most Buddhist and its ancient boundaries are marked by four grassy mounds on which are the remains of *stupas* built by Ashoka, a great Buddhist king of India (c.273-232 B.C.) who did much to spread his religion to neighbouring countries. It is not surprising that several important Buddhist buildings are found in this city. The Hiranya Varna Mahabihar is a twelfth-century building with a gold-plated roof. It is considered the most beautiful Buddhist monastery in Nepal. The Mahabouddha Temple, known as the "Temple of a Thousand Buddhas" because each brick contains an image of the Buddha, is built in the style of a structure at Bodh Gaya in India, the place where the Buddha was believed to have gained enlightenment. Near the Mahabouddha Temple is another monastery, named Rudra Varna Mahabihara, which also contains many images of the Buddha.

It must not, however, be supposed that there are no Hindu monuments in Patan. On the contrary, there are a good number of temples around Patan Durbar Square. Of these, the most notable are Krishna Mandir and the Taleju Temple. Krishna is one of the incarnations of the Hindu god Vishnu. His temple, built in the seventeenth century in an Indian style, is constructed entirely of stone without using any nails or wood. On the pillars of this temple are carved the stories of the Mahabharata and the Ramayana, two great poems of ancient India which tell the tales of heroes, gods and kings who fought the forces of evil. The Taleju Temple of Patan was built about a century later than the one at Kathmandu. It is well known for its beautiful wood-carvings. The temple of Rato Machhendranath in whose honour a festival is held every year in April is also to be found in Patan.

About ten kilometres (six miles) to the east of Kathmandu city is Bhaktipur, or Badgaon. It is smaller than either of the two other cities of the valley, but it is considered by some to be the most interesting because it has changed very little since the late seventeenth century when the greater part of it was constructed by one of the Malla kings. Bhaktipur is regarded as having three main squares: the Durbar Square, Nyatapola Square and Dattatreya Square. They are all very close to each other. At the Durbar Square are the Fifty-Five Windowed Palace (first built in the fifteenth century and renovated in the seventeenth) and the highly decorated Golden Gate, sometimes described as the finest piece of art in Nepal.

In Nyatapola Square is the Nyatapola Temple, a five-storey structure which is the tallest temple in the valley and an exceptionally fine example of Nepalese craftsmanship. It is flanked by another temple, dedicated to Bhairab, noted for having a rectangular base instead of the square one usual for buildings of this kind.

Dattatreya Temple (which dates back to the fifteenth century) is the oldest one in the area and is supposed to have been constructed from the wood of one tree, like the Kasthamandap building. Close by is the Pujahari Math, also from about the same date, with beautiful wooden carvings in the courtyard and

A view of part of Bhaktipur, one of the three cities in the Kathmandu valley

a particularly fine window carved in the likeness of a peacock.

Some way from the three cities, spread out across the valley, are yet more religious buildings, among these the two famous Buddhist *stupas* Swayambunath and Bodhnath. According to legend, way back in the past when the Kathmandu valley was one big lake, a beautiful lotus appeared under the water just above what is now the hill on which the Swayambunath *stupa* is built. From this lotus there rose a flame which represented an ancient Buddha called Swayambhu. After many years, the valley was drained by a divine saint, and the sacred hill became visible. The *stupa* of Swayambhunath was built in the time of the Lichhavis. The beautiful eyes painted on its gilt tower look calmly down on the valley. Climbing up the hill to the *stupa* one sees many monkeys. Sometimes it is called the Monkey Temple.

Bodhnath is another Buddhist *stupa,* like Swayambhunath, with tranquil eyes surveying the world. It is, however, not on top of a hill but in the middle of fields and it was built not more than five centuries ago. It has always been closely associated with Tibetan Buddhists, and many Tibetans live and work around this huge *stupa.* Swayambhunath and Bodhnath are the major centres of Buddhist activities and festivals in the Kathmandu valley.

Nyatapola Temple in Bhaktipur, the tallest temple in the Kathmandu valley

Hindus washing in the holy water of the Bagmati river at Pashupatinath

Among the other religious sites in the valley worth noting are the Pashupatinath temple, Changunarayan, Daxinkali and Budhanilkantha. Pashupati, Lord of Animals, is considered one form of the great god Shiva, and Pashupatinath is known as the most holy Hindu temple in Nepal. It is on the banks of the Bagmati river. There are also platforms here for burning the dead according to Hindu custom. The temple was first built about three centuries ago, since when there have been various renovations and additions. Most of it is open only to Hindus.

Changunarayan is a temple for the worship of Vishnu, one

of the major Hindu gods. It is situated on a hill which has been considered sacred for many centuries. The oldest stone inscription in the valley was found there. There are some images on the site which date back to about the same time—the fifth or sixth century—but the temple itself is not much more than two hundred years old.

Daxinkali is a temple of Kali, another form of the terrifying goddess Durga, and it is a place for animal sacrifices which take place on certain days of the week.

In Budhanilkantha can be found a huge image of the god Vishnu sleeping on a bed of snakes in the middle of a big water tank. It is a beautiful stone-carving which gives an impression of great strength and peace. The name can lead to confusion, for to some it sounds like the Buddha, and some Buddhists do look upon it as a form of the Buddha. Budhanilkantha means

A stone carving at Budhanilkantha of the Hindu god Vishnu sleeping on a bed of snakes

"Old Blue Throat", which might seem to suggest the god Shiva, whose throat turned blue after drinking poison. But, in fact, the image is that of the god Vishnu in one of his best-known forms—asleep on the coils of a snake (his favourite symbolic animal), floating on water (symbolizing the universe).

The Kathmandu valley is full of art treasures and important religious monuments, but it is also a place where people live and work. In fact, because there is so little room inside the closely

A colourful, crowded market scene in Kathmandu

built houses, much activity goes on in the streets and open spaces where people thresh grain, put out foodstuffs to dry, and perform other similar tasks. There is also a lot of trade and business in the valley. The most famous bazaar, called Asan Tol, is along a street that cuts diagonally across Kathmandu city.

A Nepalese bazaar is a noisy, colourful place with many little shops jammed beside each other, most of them forming part of traditional Newar-style houses, which have a slightly higgledy-piggledy look. For all its beauty and interest, Kathmandu is not a place noted for cleanliness and there are many parts where basic sanitation does not exist.

Since Nepal opened its doors to the world, many visitors and tourists have travelled there, prominent among them "hippies", and other westerners, trying to find a way of life different from what they have known in their own countries. There is hardly any place in the valley today where foreigners are not to be seen. Among the medieval buildings there are now modern hotels, restaurants, curio shops and other signs of a country that relies heavily on tourism. It is a jumble of twentieth-century life and old traditions. Sometimes it is difficult to decide which is the more interesting, the past or the present.

Exploring the Country

Few people go to the land of Mount Everest without hoping to catch a glimpse of the world's highest mountain. Everest has fascinated climbers ever since it became known to the western world in the late nineteenth century. Attempts to complete the ascent of this massive mountain began in the 1920s. However, it was only in 1953 that two men from a British team reached the summit—Edmund Hilary (a New Zealander) and Tenzin Norgay (a Sherpa). Since then, many other expeditions have managed to scale the peak, but it still continues to attract climbers from all over the world. Apart from this most famous of mountains, there are other peaks in the Nepal Himalayas which are difficult of access and present an exciting challenge. Mountaineering has therefore become one of the pursuits which bring money and publicity to Nepal, with teams of climbers arriving every year.

For those who either cannot or do not wish to climb mountains, but who want to enjoy the beauties of its countryside, Nepal offers the pleasures of trekking—walking along mountain trails for days or weeks, alone or as part of a group. This is now so popular among foreign visitors that there are agencies which will make all the arrangements for a good trek. The cost can be quite high, depending on how well you want to live on

A view of Mount Everest, the world's highest mountain

the trek and where you want to go. For those who do not wish to spend too much money it is possible to go off on their own without a guide and without much equipment, making do with whatever food and shelter they can carry on their backs or find along the trail. This kind of one-man show enables a trekker to get to know the land and the people, and can turn out to be a wonderful experience. However, it can also be a disaster if proper care is not taken over the arrangements.

The most important thing for all mountaineering and trekking expeditions is to have an efficient, reliable Sherpa guide who knows the route, who can see to all the little details of life on the trail and who, above all, can manage the porters. Following tracks where no car can go and spending days or even weeks far from any place where necessities can be bought means that even one person might need several porters to carry his or her camping gear. Foreigners are often surprised by the size of the loads which the Nepalese porters, who are usually quite small, can carry up and down hills for many hours at a stretch. Sometimes porters may decide that they do not wish to go on,

A Sherpa porter carrying a heavy load over a bridge in the foothills of the Himalayas

Sherpas cooking a mid-morning meal for a group of trekkers in the foothills of the Himalayas. Trekking and mountaineering now provide jobs and livelihood for many Nepalese

either because they are sick, or because they have made enough money, or because they do not have enough clothes to keep them warm once they get up to the colder altitudes. At these times, much depends on the guide's ability either to persuade them to stay on, or to hire new porters, or to redistribute the loads among those willing to remain.

The honesty, efficiency and pleasantness of Sherpas in the face of emergencies under difficult conditions have been praised by many who have climbed and trekked in Nepal. But, in recent years, there have also been complaints that the Sherpas are getting spoilt and greedy. There may be a certain amount of truth in such criticism, but it has to be remembered that many changes in Sherpa life have been brought about by contact with foreigners who have little understanding of local circumstances. Foreigners are rich by comparison with Nepalese and they often behave with little regard for the feelings and customs of the local population. It is not surprising that they have come to be looked upon as sources of income rather than as visitors to be treated with the natural good manners and friendliness for which the Nepalese have been known.

A climber wishing to attempt one of the mountains of Nepal would have to join an expedition. All arrangements, in particular getting permission from the Nepalese government, have to be made well in advance. People interested in trekking, however, can wait until they get to Nepal before deciding where and how they will explore the mountain trails, according to their own interests. Some trekkers hope to discover the wide variety of bird-life and so may wish to proceed slowly, taking photographs, recording all the species they come across. Some may be more interested in plants and wild flowers, or in the customs of the local peoples, or simply in getting a good walk done in as short a time as possible. Nepal has much to offer and there is something to satisfy almost any taste.

In the past few decades since tourism became one of the major money-earners of the country, a number of popular treks have come to be recognized. The best known of these is perhaps the trek to the Everest base camp in eastern Nepal. It is not a very easy route and takes about three weeks, beginning from the usual

Yaks at the Everest base camp in eastern Nepal. This is one of the most popular treks

starting-point at Lamosangu. It is possible to shorten the trip by flying from Kathmandu to Lukla, only a few days' walk from the Everest base camp. Going the long way one passes through areas inhabited by different Nepalese peoples, such as the Tamangs and Rais, although Everest itself is in Sherpa country. In this district, known as Solu Khumbu, the Tibetan character of Sherpa life can be seen clearly, particularly at the Buddhist monastery of Thangboche, which is a famous landmark. It is a large, sprawling structure in Tibetan style. One of its interesting treasures is a skull, supposedly of a yeti.

Another popular trek is the one that goes from the Kathmandu valley to the foot of the Langtang peak in the north. The route

The Buddhist monastery of Thangboche in the district of Solu Khumbu. It is rumoured that its treasures include the skull of a yeti

passes through Tamang and Tibetan villages and takes about two weeks. For those who are willing and able, it is possible to climb up to a sacred lake called Gosainkund. Hindus make pilgrimages there, especially at the time of the August full moon. The Helambu region also lies north of Kathmandu and a trek to this area is suitable for those who do not want to be on the trail too long. This is again Sherpa country, and may also include a trip to the lake of Gosainkund.

To the west of Kathmandu is the valley of Pokhara, which lies in the shadow of the famous Annapurna range and the beautiful mountain of Macchapuchare. The view of the peaks from the valley is dazzling, and a number of popular treks can be undertaken with Pokhara as the starting-point. The one which goes to the little town of Jomosom is often considered the most interesting in Nepal because the route passes through different landscapes and crosses the Himalayas between Annapurna and Daulagiri along the world's deepest river gorge.

The more adventurous traveller might prefer a trek west of the Kali Gandaki river. It costs more to explore these areas where there are few roads, little food available for visitors and long distances to be covered. Those expecting magnificent views of the Himalayas will be disappointed, but there are other attractions. The vegetation is interesting and, unlike most areas in the east, the forests have remained largely unspoilt. The inhabitants of the west have not yet had much contact with the

A view of the Annapurna range to the west of Kathmandu

modern world. They lead a more traditional way of life than those who live within easier reach of visitors. One of the most popular treks in western Nepal is the one which leaves from the town of Jumla and climbs up to Rara, the largest lake in Nepal, lying at a height of 3,050 metres (nearly 10,000 feet).

There are many people who choose to leave the beaten track, either because they prefer to go where few others have been or because their interests lie in certain special geographical or cultural areas, but it is not possible for foreigners to visit all parts of Nepal. Many areas outside the Kathmandu valley require special permits. And, while these can easily be obtained for some places, there are others near the northern border which are entirely closed to foreigners.

Exploring the mountain trails of Nepal can be an exciting and rewarding experience for the visitor. In addition, trekking and mountaineering provide jobs and livelihoods for many Nepalese. However, these pastimes have also created problems along the popular routes, not the least of which is pollution. Carelessly used camp sites, the unthinking destruction of trees and wildlife, and the spread of litter are some of the things which threaten the beauty of Nepal's scenery.

For those who find jungles more interesting than mountains, Nepal also has something to offer. Ninety-seven kilometres (sixty miles) south-west of Kathmandu is the Chitwan National Park, nearly 520 square kilometres (more than two hundred square miles) in area and full of big game. It is not so usual for visitors to trek in this area, partly because facilities are poor and partly

Trekkers enjoying a well-earned break. Many tourists now flock to Nepal every year to go mountaineering or walking and to see for themselves something of Nepal's rich natural and cultural heritage

because the weather tends to be too hot for long walks to be pleasant. There are agencies which arrange trips to Chitwan, and the park can be reached by air from Kathmandu. The Tiger Tops Jungle Lodge is a well-known and expensive hotel where those who can afford it enjoy "jungle living" in safety and comfort. The lodge will plan boat-trips, elephant-rides and animal-watching. Bait is put out at night to attract the tigers and leopards, and guests can view these from specially built hides. Those who find the jungle lodge too expensive can go to the Elephant Camp or the Gaida Wildlife Camp in other parts of the park. Accommodation there is in tents and, although not so luxurious as Tiger Tops, there are equal chances for seeing a good number of wild animals. Canoeing, boating, swimming and fishing during the season are other pleasures the park offers to visitors.

Chitwan is the best known national park in Nepal, but there are four others which include the Everest area, Lake Rara, Dolpo and Langtang. October to November and February to April are considered the most pleasant seasons for exploring the country, while the monsoon months (June to September) are best avoided.

It is important for visitors who want to venture outside the Kathmandu valley to take proper medical precautions. A trip which has cost a lot of money to arrange and which could have been a wonderful experience can easily be spoilt by ill health or accident in areas where doctors and hospitals are not available.

Facing the Future

It is easy to be so fascinated by Nepal's colourful life and so impressed by the beauty of its Himalayan landscape that the difficulties of life in this little kingdom are overlooked. Foreigners see the Nepalese people as cheerful and content. In fact, their life is very hard and, not unnaturally, they long for a share in the wealth which rich visitors display in abundance.

Nepal earns most of its foreign exchange from tourism: more than 200,000 tourists flock to the country each year and the number is on the increase. In the face of this great inrush, Nepal has felt the need to adjust to the modern world at full speed. Most nations made the change from a medieval-type society to the twentieth century in slow stages, taking time to adjust to new ideas and discoveries. Nepal, by contrast, has had to progress to modern statehood in such a hurry that it has barely had time to stop to take stock. Because they see that their standard of living is far behind those of the rich, developed nations, the Nepalese are impatient to get ahead as quickly as they can.

When people from the developed world come to Nepal, they are eager to see or even experience a way of life that is quite different from what they know in their own countries. For the majority of them Nepal is rather like a museum; they hope it

A Tibetan woman milking a yak. Yaks are also commonly used as beasts of burden in Nepal

will change as little as possible. But living in a museum is not entirely desirable. The Nepalese would much rather enjoy the comforts that come with modern technology and development. At the same time, they do not wish to lose all their traditions or a sense of pride in their own culture. It is very much a question of striking the right balance.

To achieve progress without losing what is good and worth preserving is a basic concern of the Nepalese government. It also has the task of protecting the rich cultural heritage that has been handed down through the centuries. This is not always easy. The preservation of old buildings requires money and skill which are not always available. The preservation of art objects presents another problem. Visitors to Nepal naturally wish to buy souvenirs to take home and there are many interesting and attractive examples of local handicrafts to be found in Kathmandu. However, some foreigners are more ambitious; they try to acquire rare antiques which it is forbidden by law to take out of the country. There is a great temptation for poor people to sell off (or exchange for modern gadgets) some old object which might have been in their families for generations. There are also those who steal religious images, paintings and manuscripts from temples and monasteries because they know they can find foreigners who will pay well for such things. The smuggling out of art treasures is one of the prices that Nepal

A village street in northern Nepal. Although much of Nepal seems backward by western standards, the government is keen to ensure that modernization will not destroy the country's traditions

A woman wearing jewellery of silver, coral and turquoise, much sought after by foreigners

is having to pay for opening its doors to the modern world.

On the other hand, there are many western individuals and institutions who are keen to help Nepal preserve the wealth of fine craftsmanship which has come down from the past. For example, the government of the German Democratic Republic is helping with a programme to restore the city of Bhaktipur; it is also engaged in a project to microfilm old Nepalese manuscripts. Foreign scholars and writers have played a part in promoting an interest in Nepalese culture and history. In this, as in much else, there are areas for useful international co-operation.

Not all parts of Nepal have developed equally, and there is

a movement away from the hills towards the Terai and other centres where modern industries provide jobs. The decreasing population of the more sparsely inhabited areas brings the danger of their falling even further behind the comparatively developed parts of the country. The government is trying to improve the situation by launching a national "back-to-the-village" campaign. People are encouraged to stay in the villages and take part in the progress of the country through the *panchayat* system. But the government's efforts have not met with too much success because the opportunities which towns offer for making money act as a strong magnet for those who can no longer make a living from the land. Moving from a village to a more developed centre means leaving behind the traditional supports of family ties and long-established customs which small communities provide. Often it is a great hardship for villagers to live and work in alien surroundings among strangers, but the need for employment drives them to it.

The government of Nepal under King Birendra is not unaware of the need to distinguish between modernization merely for the sake of modernization and modernization for the sake of progress. However, the government itself is also under some pressure to make changes in keeping with the idea of progress. In spite of the *panchayat* system which allows the people to have some say in the way in which their country is run and, in spite of the genuine concern of the king for the welfare of the people, there is much political discontent. Many educated Nepalese feel that their country should have a more democratic form of government and, unless the king can gain their support, there could be political disturbances in the future.

But what kind of future can be expected for a small country struggling against poverty and trying to defend its independence and internal unity? Judging from its record over the past three decades, there is reason to be optimistic. Nepal has shown a capacity to tackle her problems with resolution and good sense. In spite of the mistakes she may have made in the past, there seems little doubt that she will be able to face the future with confidence and dignity.

Index

Abominable Snowman, *see* yeti
Afghanistan 12
animal sacrifice, *see* blood sacrifice
Annapurna 12, 14, 53, 82
architecture 62-4
Aryans 36
Asan Tol 75
Ashoka 68
Asia 62

Badgaon 69
Bagmati river 67, 72
Bala Chaturdasi 41, 47
Bhairab 41, 66
    Kalo (Black) Bhairab 66-7
    Sweta (White) Bhairab 67
Bhaktipur 20, 69, 90
Bhotias 56-8
Bihar 55
birds 15
Birendra, King 30, 91
blood sacrifice 45, 48
Bodh Gaya 68
Bodhnath 70, 71
Bodos 54
Brahmins 36, 50
Britain 12
British 23
British army 23, 52
British East India Company 22-3
Buddha 17, 38-9, 63, 68
Buddhism 11, 20, 36-9, 56-7
Buddhism, Tibetan, *see* Tibetan Buddhism
Buddhist art and culture 11
Buddhist images and monuments 40, 63, 68
Buddhist religious days 41
Buddhists 12, 17, 19, 40, 41, 43, 50, 53, 71

Budhanilkantha 72, 73-4
Burma 12

caste system 36-9
chaitan, see *stupa*
Changunarayan 72
Chhetris 50
China 7, 34
Chinese 22, 49, 58
Chitwan National Park 9, 84-6
Cho-Oyu 12
clothing 59-60
communications 31-3

Danwars 54
Darais 54
Dasain 41, 44-6
Dattatreya Square 69
Daulagiri 12, 14
Daxinkali 72, 73
development 9, 30-35
Dhimals 54
diet 60-61
Divali 41, 46
Dolpo 58, 86
Durbar Square, Bhaktipur 69
Durbar Square, Kathmandu 43, 64-6
Durbar Square, Patan 68
Durga 42, 45, 73
Durga Puja 41, 45

economy 9, 30
education 31-2
Elephant Camp 85
Everest, Mount 12, 57, 76, 80-81, 86

festivals 40-48
food crops 11, 30

Gaida Wildlife Camp 85
Ganges, river 9
Gangetic dolphin 9
geography 7-15

German Democratic Republic 90
Gorkha 21, 22, 53
Gorkha kings 21, 23
Gorkhalis 23
Gosainkund 82
government 9, 28-30, 91
Gurkhas 23, 26, 52, 54, 59
Gurungs 53-4

Hanuman Dhoka 42, 64-5
health 31, 33
Helambu 82
Hilary, Edmund 76
Himalayan griffon vulture 15
Himalayas 8-10, 12-16, 62, 76, 83
Hindu arts and culture 11
Hindu festivals 40-48
Hindu monarchy 7, 17
Hindu shrines 47, 65, 68-9, 72-3
Hinduism 11, 20, 36-9, 45
Hindus 12, 17, 19, 36-8, 50, 53, 67, 72, 82
Hiranya Varna Mahabihar 68
history 17-27
Holi 41, 47-8
housing 61

India 7, 8, 9, 17, 21, 24, 26, 34, 36, 38, 47, 50, 55, 63, 68
Indians 17, 19, 36, 49
Indian army 23, 52
Indian government 26-7
Indo-Aryan languages 49, 50
Indo-Nepalese peoples 49
Indra 41
Indra Jatra 41-2, 44, 50, 67
Inner Himalayas 12

Jirels 54
Jomosom 83
Jumla 84
Jung Bahadur Rana, *see* Rana

Kali 73
Kali Gandaki river 14, 83
Kalo Bhairab, *see* Bhairab
Kanchenjunga 12
Kantipur 65
Kasthamandap 65, 69
Kathmandu city 20, 21, 42, 43, 62-67, 69, 75, 89
Kathmandu valley 10-11, 18, 20-21, 23, 40-42, 47, 49-51, 53, 62-75, 81-2, 84, 86
Khrishna Mandir 68
Kirantis 51-2
Koches 54-5
Kshatriyas 36, 50
Kumari 42-4, 65
Kumari Chowk 65

Lalitpur 67
lamas 52
Lamjung Himalayas 53
Lamosangu 81
Langtang 81, 86
Laxmi 46
Lichhavi kings 17-19, 52, 70
Limbu 51-2
literacy 32
Living Goddess, *see* Kumari
Lukla 81
Lumbini 38

Macchapuchare 12, 82
Machhendranath 41
Rato (red) Machhendranath 41, 69
Mahabharat Lekh 8-10
Mahabouddha Temple 68
Mahayana 57
Mahendra, King 28-30
Mahisasura 45
Magars 54
Majhis 54
Maju Deval 65

Makalu 12
malarial eradication programme 8
Malla kings 18-22, 63-4, 68-9
Manaslu 12
metal works 11
mining 11
Mongolians 49, 50-54
mountaineering 76-80, 84
Muslim conquest of India 18, 20
Muslims 18-20, 55
Mustang 58

Nepali 50
Nepal midlands 8, 10, 14, 49, 51-2, 54
Newar art 50
Newar houses 61, 64-5, 75
Newari 50
Newaris (Newars) 43, 50, 51
Norgay, see Tenzin Norgay
Nyatapola Square 69

panchayats 29-30, 91
Pashupati 72
Pashupatinath 47, 72
Patan 20, 41, 67-9
peoples 49-61
Pokhara 11, 82
politics 26-30, 91
population 33-4
Prithvi Narayan Shah 21

Rai 51-2, 81
Rajbansis 54-5
Rajendra Bikram Shah, King 24
Rajputs 21, 54
Rama 45
Rana family 7, 26-8, 30
Rana, Jung Bahadur 24-6
Rara, Lake 84, 86
Rato Machhendranath, see Machendranath

Ravana 45
religion 11, 36-40
Rudra Varna Mahabihara 68

Sanskrit 17
Santals 55
Satars 54
sattal 65
Shah kings 23-4, 26, 53, 64
Shakya caste 43
Sherpas 57-8, 76-82
Shiva 45, 72, 73
Siddhartha 38
Siwalik Hills (Siwaliks) 8-9
Solu Khumbu 81
State Kumari, see Kumari
stupa 63, 70-71
Sudras 36
Sunwars 54
Sweta Bhairab, see Bhairab
Swayambunath 17, 70-71

Taleju Temple 65, 68
Tamangs 52-3, 56, 81-2
Tantras 39
Tantric practices 57
Tenzin Norgay 76
Terai 8-9, 15, 49, 52, 54-6, 91
Thakalis 54
Thangboche 81
Tharus 54
Tibet 17, 20-22, 50-52, 56-8
Tibetan Buddhism 52-3, 56-7, 71
Tibetan Marginal Mountains 12
Tibetan plateau 10, 12-13, 22, 52, 56, 71
Tibetans 81-2
Tibeto-Nepalese peoples 49
Tibeto-Burman languages, peoples 49, 50-51, 54
Tiger Tops Jungle Lodge 85
Tihar, see Divali

tika 45
tourism 75, 80, 87
transport 32-3
trekking 76-84
Tribhuvan, King 7, 27-8

UNESCO 65
untouchables, *see* Sudras

Vaishyas 36
Vishnu 68, 72-4
Vishnumati river 67

wildlife 9, 15, 85

Yama 46
yeti 16